A Kalmus Classic Edition

Johannes

KALLIWODA

SIX NOCTURNES

Opus 186

Urtext Edition

FOR VIOLA AND PIANO

K 04330

Notturno I.

Notturno I.
J. W. Kalliwoda, Op. 186.
con espressione
Larghetto.
Viola.
Larghetto.
Pianoforte.
A
B
EDWIN F. KALMUS
PUBLISHER OF MUSIC
NEW YORK, N.Y.

C
grandioso
f
ff
mf
m.s.

D

6
E
p
F.
p
f
G dolce
p
ten.
pp
ritard.
ritard.
p
p
sempre di - mi - nu - en - do
pp
pp

Notturno II.

Allegretto, ma un poco vivo.
Allegretto, ma un poco vivo.
mf
p leggiero
sempre cre - - - - scen - - -
di f
f
p
p
A
B

C
mf
f
p
D
f
f
p
f
f

Notturno III.

C
dolce
ritard.
ritard.
D
p
f
f
f
p
f
p
ff
ff
E
p
p
p

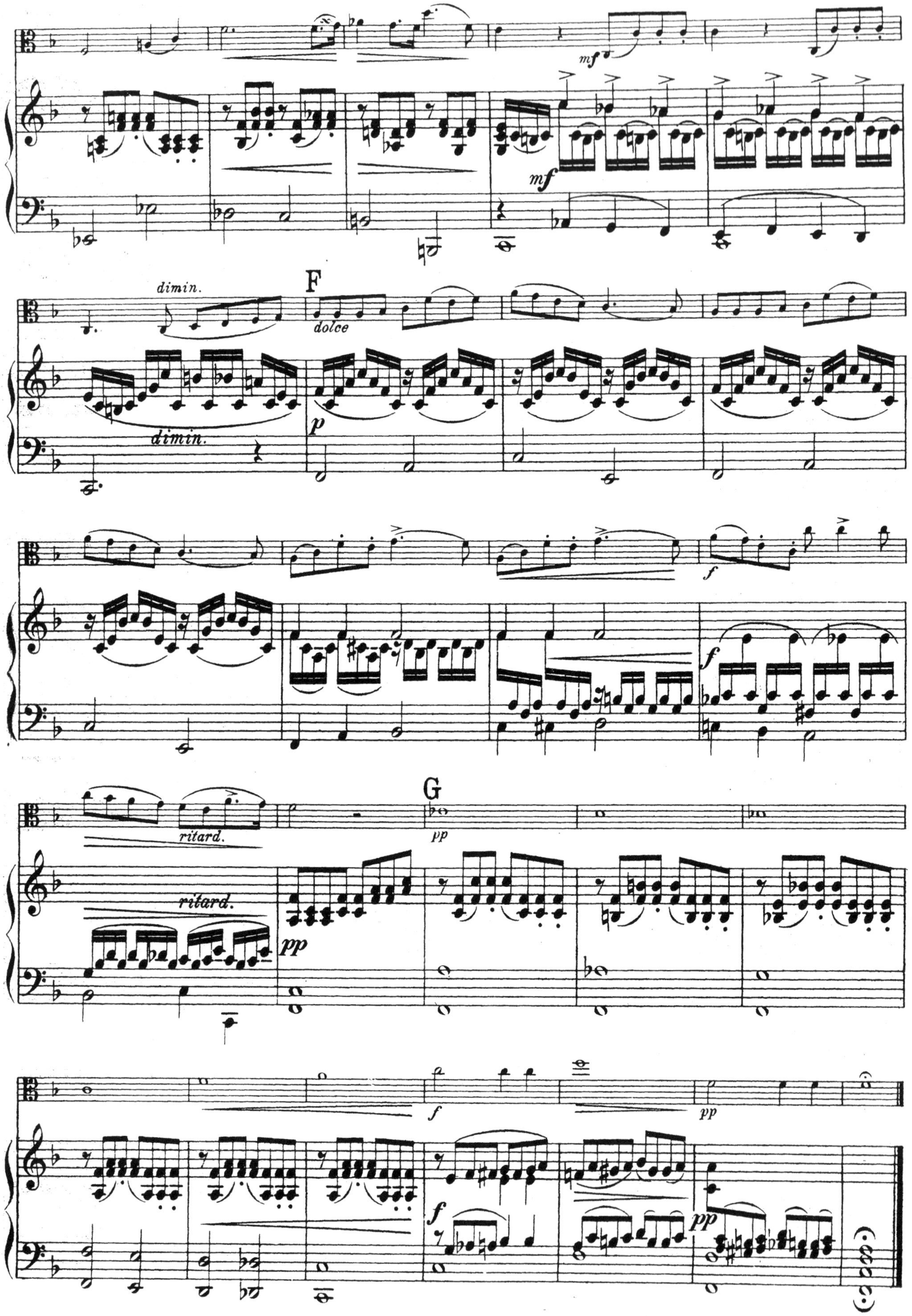
mf
mf
dimin.
F
dolce
dimin.
p
f
f
G
ritard.
ritard.
pp
pp
f
f
pp
pp

Notturno IV.

C
D
dolce
p
cre - - - scen

Six Nocturnes.

VIOLA.

Larghetto.
con espressione

J. W. Kalliwoda, Op. 186.

№ 1.

VIOLA.

F
G
p dolce
ritard.
sempre di _ mi _ nu _ en _ do
Allegretto, ma un poco vivo.
№ 2.
mf
A
sempre cre _ _ scen _ _
_ do f
B
p
V
f
C
mf
D
f
p
f
E
f
p

VIOLA.
3
F
G
H
I
K
L

VIOLA.

Poco Adagio.
cantabile
№ 3.
p
A
B
dolce
f
ritard.
D
f
ff
E
p
dimin.
F
dolce
mf
G
ritard.
pp
f
pp

VIOLA.

Allegretto, ma un poco vivo.
Nº 4.
A
B
C
D
dolce
cre _ _ scen _ _ do
E
F
ritard.
G in tempo
H

VIOLA.

I
K
L
M
N
sempre di_mi_nu_en_do
Adagio con molta espressione.
№ 5.
ritard.
A
cantabile
B
C grandioso

con molta espressione
dolce
f
p
f
p
f
ritard.
F
E
D
dolce
f
p
H
p
p
di _ mi _ nu _ en _ do
Allegro moderato.
№ 6.
Pfte.
f
A
B
p
C
f
G

VIOLA.
dolce
D
ritard.
E
di_mi_nu_en_do
f
F
p
G
f
H
I
K
p
ritard. L
ff

E
do
f
p
p
F
p
p

ritard.
G in tempo
in tempo
ritard.
f
p
p
H
f
f

M
N
sempre diminuendo
sempre diminuendo

Notturno V.

Adagio con molta espressione.
Adagio con molta espressione.
p
ritard.
ritard.
A
cantabile
f
f
p

22
B
C
grandioso
cre - - - scen - - do
f
p
ff
3
6

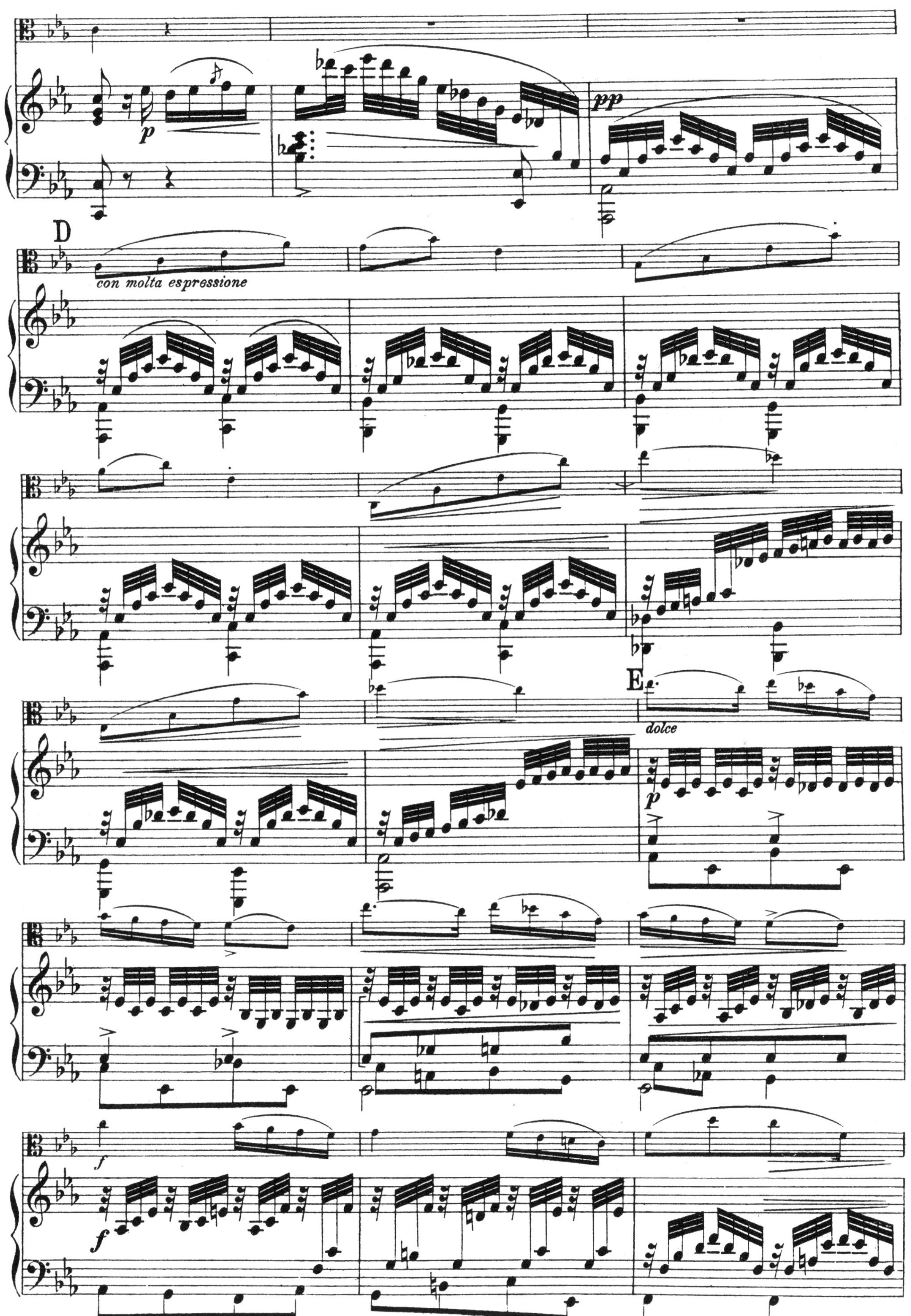
con molta espressione
pp
p
D
dolce
E
p
f
f

f
f
H
p
pp
p
p
di - mi - nu - en - do
di - mi - nu - en - do

Notturno VI.

B
C
dolce
p
p
p
f
f
p

28
D
E
ritard.
nuen - do
ritard.
f
ff
f
p
pp
p
f
ff
p
pp
di - mi -
f

F
p
p
ritard.

G
H
I
f
f

K
p
p
f
f
f
p
ritard.
p
ritard.
L
ff
ff